DILLY GOES
TO THE DENTIST

TONY BRADMAN

DILLY GOES

TO THE DENTIST

Illustrated by Susan Hellard

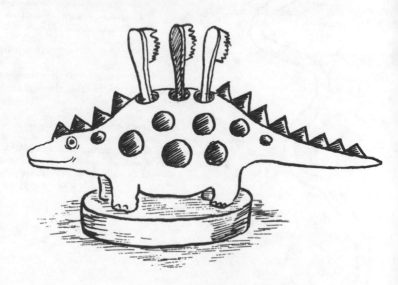

PUFFIN BOOKS

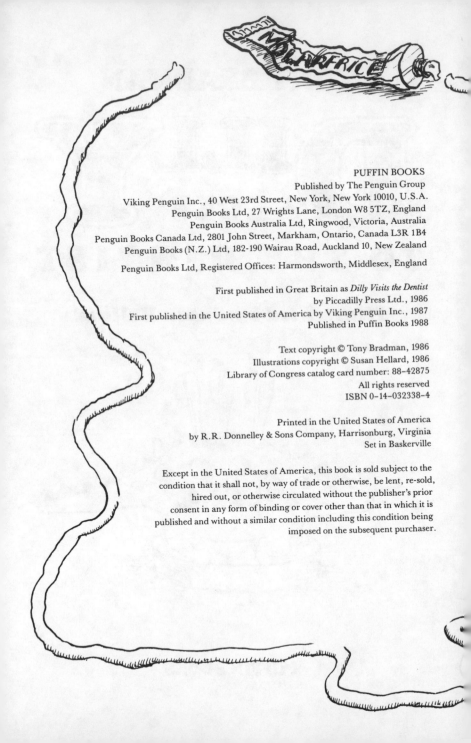

PUFFIN BOOKS
Published by The Penguin Group
Viking Penguin Inc., 40 West 23rd Street, New York, New York 10010, U.S.A.
Penguin Books Ltd, 27 Wrights Lane, London W8 5TZ, England
Penguin Books Australia Ltd, Ringwood, Victoria, Australia
Penguin Books Canada Ltd, 2801 John Street, Markham, Ontario, Canada L3R 1B4
Penguin Books (N.Z.) Ltd, 182-190 Wairau Road, Auckland 10, New Zealand

Penguin Books Ltd, Registered Offices: Harmondsworth, Middlesex, England

First published in Great Britain as *Dilly Visits the Dentist*
by Piccadilly Press Ltd., 1986
First published in the United States of America by Viking Penguin Inc., 1987
Published in Puffin Books 1988

Text copyright © Tony Bradman, 1986
Illustrations copyright © Susan Hellard, 1986
Library of Congress catalog card number: 88-42875
All rights reserved
ISBN 0-14-032338-4

Printed in the United States of America
by R.R. Donnelley & Sons Company, Harrisonburg, Virginia
Set in Baskerville

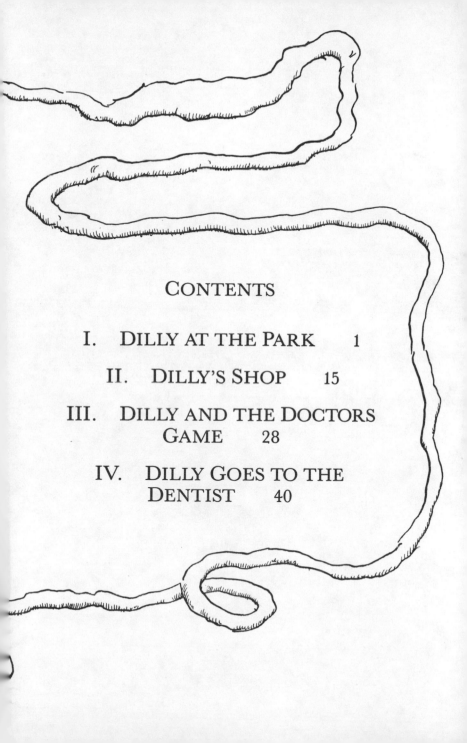

CONTENTS

DILLY
GOES
TO THE DENTIST

I. DILLY AT THE PARK

You've all heard about Dilly Dinosaur and his ultra-special, 150-mile-per-hour super-scream, haven't you? You haven't? I thought everyone knew about Dilly!

Well, my name's Dorla, and Dilly is my little brother. We live with our mother and father, and most of the time we're very happy. But when Dilly is naughty, or when he's stubborn, or when he's so cross that he lets loose

1

that ultra-special super-scream of
his—then the Dinosaur family isn't so
happy.

In fact, not so very long ago, Dilly
was having one of his bad days. And
when he has a day like that, there's no
other little dinosaur in the world who
can behave as badly as our Dilly can.

He stomped and sulked and
shouted. He sulked and screamed and
pouted. He screamed and pouted and
stomped. Mother and Father kept
telling him off, but it didn't seem to

make any difference. So I decided to keep out of his way until he felt like being nicer.

I sat in my room reading for a while, when suddenly I heard the sound we had all been dreading. The windows rattled, the floor shook and— BONK—the handle fell off my door.

Dilly had fired off an ultra-special, 150-mile-per-hour super-scream. What was the matter now?

I went downstairs and into the kitchen. Dilly was standing in front of the table with his arms crossed. By his feet there was a broken cup, and a puddle of spilled juice. I could see that he had his I'm-going-to-sulk-as-hard-as-I-can look on his face, too.

Dilly had stopped screaming, but Mother still had her ears covered and her eyes shut.

"He's not screaming any more, Mother," I said. She opened her eyes and looked at Dilly very crossly.

"Well!" she said. "And what have you got to say for yourself now, Dilly Dinosaur?" But Dilly didn't say anything.

It turned out that Dilly had thrown his cup down in a temper because he couldn't have his own way. He wanted to go to the park, and Mother had said no.

"If you had just let me finish what I was saying, Dilly," she said, "I would have told you that we were going to the park *after lunch*. But now I'm not so sure I will take you, because you've been such a bad dinosaur."

Now Dilly loves going to the park more than almost anywhere else. When he heard what Mother said, I could see that he wanted to cry. But I could also see that he still wanted to sulk. His face couldn't make up its mind whether to sulk or cry, so it was doing some very funny things instead.

But I wasn't very happy either. I wanted to go to the park too. I wanted to try out the new roller skates I got for my birthday. And if Mother didn't take Dilly because he had been bad, she wouldn't be able to take me, either.

Dilly's face finally made up its mind. Dilly started to cry.

"It's no use crying, Dilly," said Mother. "What's done is done. That is . . . unless you're sorry?"

Dilly stopped crying. He nodded.

"And do you promise to clear up the mess you've made on the floor?"

Dilly nodded harder still, and kept nodding.

"Okay, Dilly," said Mother. "We can go to the park. And stop nodding like that, you're giving me a headache."

Dilly was pleased that we were going to the park, and so was I. In fact, Dilly was so pleased he promised to be as good as gold, and I have to say that he behaved very well all through lunch. Why, he didn't throw any food at me, and he didn't say "Yuk!" all the time like he usually does. He ate everything up—even his fern stalks and swamp greens.

The only time he looked a little cross was after lunch, when Mother said he couldn't ride his dino-trike to the park.

"Now you know what you're like, Dilly," she said. "You go crashing into things and falling off. I'll carry your dino-trike and you can ride it when we get there. Dorla's not going to put her skates on until we're in the park, either."

It was a lovely day, and the park was full of dinosaurs. Dilly wanted to go on the tree swings first, and then on the rock slide, and then on the log roundabout, and then on the swings again. I put my roller skates on and

went up and down the track by the swamp.

"Be careful, Dorla," Mother called out. The truth is that I'm still not very good on my skates. I'm a little wobbly on them in fact, and I don't go very fast. But I'm getting better.

Anyway, after a while, Dilly decided that he wanted to ride his dino-trike. He tore up and down the track making all the other dinosaurs jump out of his way.

"Dilly!" shouted Mother. "Will you stop that!"

Dilly took no notice, although he did look round at her.

"Dilly!" she called out. "Watch where you're going! You'll end up in the swamp!"

It was true. Dilly was heading straight for the edge of the swamp but

he swerved and crashed into a giant
fern before he got there. Mother ran
up to him, and I came along behind.
Dilly was crying because he'd grazed
his leg.

"Perhaps that will teach you to slow down," said Mother. She gave him a hug, kissed his leg better, and soon he was up and riding on his dino-trike again.

I was trying hard to roller-skate properly. I went up and down the track by the swamp very slowly. Mother said I was beginning to look quite good at skating, but it didn't feel

like it.

Dilly was going up and down the track making very loud "brmm-brmmm" noises. He went in and out of everybody's legs and once he nearly bumped into an old dinosaur, who looked rather cross. Mother didn't notice Dilly do that, but I did.

Then Dilly started to chase me.

He flew up the track on his dino-trike, skidded round, and came tearing down towards me. From the look on his face I could see that he was going to try and knock me over! And do you know, he was laughing!

Well, what could I do? I didn't think I was clever enough on my skates to get out of his way without falling over. But just as he was about to crash into me I grabbed the tree I was going past. I swung right round it while

Dilly flew off . . . straight towards the swamp!

And this time he didn't swerve. He went in a straight line . . . and with a great KER-PLOP and SQUELCH . . . he went straight in, head first.

I fell over then, and it took me a while to get back on my skates. So when I got over to Dilly, Mother was already in the swamp up to her knees, trying to get him out. All I could see of him was his tail and his feet, and it

took Mother quite a lot of time to pull him out of the nasty-smelling mud.

Mother was very cross with him.

"Dilly Dinosaur," she said, "will you look at my shoes . . . and my legs . . . and as for my dress . . . well!"

Mother did look very messy from the waist down. But she didn't look as messy as Dilly. He was covered in mud from head to foot, and the only clean bit of him that I could see was the very tip of his tail.

Dilly looked so funny, standing there all muddy and wet and bedraggled, that I couldn't stop laughing. Mother joined in, and even Dilly began to giggle when he started to walk, and heard himself squelching.

And do you know what Dilly said later on when he was in the bath?

"Mother," he said, "Mother, can I

have a pair of roller skates like
Dorla's?"

Mother gave Dilly a hard look.
"I don't know about that, Dilly,"
she said. "I really don't."

II. DILLY'S SHOP

The other day, when Father was
making breakfast, Dilly started asking
questions. He's been doing that a lot
recently, and sometimes it can be
pretty annoying.

"Where does money come from,
Father?" Dilly asked.

Father looked very hot and
bothered. The eggs were boiling in the
pan, the fern stalks were burning
under the grill, and he had dropped

the butter on the floor.

"What, Dilly?" he said. "Where does money come from? It certainly doesn't grow on giant ferns." He knelt down and started to scrape the butter off the floor.

"I know that, Father," said Dilly. "But where does it come from? Does it come from the bank?"

Father laughed. He stopped what he was doing and looked up at Dilly.

"Well, it comes from the bank, all right, but only if you put some in there first."

Dilly looked confused.

"But where does it come from, then? How do you get it?" he asked.

"That's quite a difficult question to answer, Dilly," said Father. "I suppose most people get it by going to work. They get paid for doing a job."

16

Dilly looked even more confused.

"But Dorla doesn't go to work," said Dilly, "she only goes to school."

"That's right," said Father. Now he was looking confused. "I don't see . . ."

"But Dorla's got some money," said Dilly. "She showed it to me this morning."

"Ah," said Father. "I see . . . well, Dilly, that's because Dorla gets pocket money, and you don't."

I could see that Dilly wasn't very happy about that.

"Why does Dorla get pocket money and not me?" he said. "I've got just as many pockets as she has." Dilly pulled out both the pockets of his dungarees to show what he meant, and everything that was in them came tumbling out. There was a snail, a few

marbles and lots of other stuff which
fell to the floor. The snail landed in the
butter that Father was trying to scrape
up.

"Do you think we could talk about
this after breakfast, Dilly?" said
Father.

Dilly thought for a moment.

"Okay," he said, at last, and sat at the table.

Dilly behaved all through breakfast. He didn't talk, he just concentrated on eating. But as soon as he had chewed and swallowed his very last mouthful, he started asking questions again.

"So why does Dorla get pocket money and I don't? And when am I going to get some? And how much can I have? And . . ."

"Hold on there a minute," said Father, "just hold on, Dilly."

I could see that Dilly had lots more questions he wanted to ask . . . but he shut up and sat with his lips firmly together, waiting to hear what Father had to say.

"First of all, up to now, Mother and I thought you were too young to have pocket money," said Father.

"But . . ." Dilly started to say. Father gave him a hard look. Dilly shut up.

"But now your mother and I agree that you're old enough to have a little pocket money every week, but only if you help out around the house, like Dorla does. We thought that your job could be to set the table at mealtimes—okay?"

Well, Dilly is usually fed up or angry about something when he brings everything to a standstill with his ultra-special, 150-mile-per-hour super-scream. This time he used it because he was pleased, although the result was the same. Mother ran out of the back door, Father ran upstairs, and I hid under the table.

When he was quiet, Father and
Mother came back into the kitchen.

"Now, Dilly," said Father, "you're
going to have to learn about how to use
your pocket money. You can save it, or
you can spend it. But remember, once
it's gone, it's gone."

"Where do you spend it?" asked
Dilly.

"In places like the Shopping
Cavern, where you buy toys or sugar
cane or grown-up things, silly Dilly," I
said.

"Now, Dorla," said Mother. "Don't
be like that. Dilly's got to learn about
those things, just as you did."

Dilly looked at Father.

"You mean if I go into a shop and give them my money," he said, "they'll give me things?"

"That's right," said Father, "so long as you give them enough money."

Dilly had his thoughtful look on his face.

"So if I had a shop, people would give me money for things?" he said.

Mother and Father laughed.

"That's right, Dilly," said Father. "Oh, and here's your pocket money." Dilly looked at the shiny coin and smiled. "Now run along and play, you two," said Father.

A little later I heard Dilly call Mother and Father up to his room. He said he had something special to show them. I went along as well to see what he was up to.

I peeked round from behind Mother and Father, and saw that Dilly was standing beside a cardboard box he'd found. On top of the box were a few of his things. There was his teddy bear, some toy dino-cars, a book, some building rocks and some other stuff. Everything had a little piece of paper

stuck on it, and on each piece of paper Dilly had scribbled something.

"Well," said Father, "this looks like a good game, Dilly. What are you playing?"

Dilly smiled his biggest I'm-really-pleased-with-myself smile.

"I'm playing shops," he said. "This is my shop, and these are the things you've got to buy."

"Oh, I see," said Mother. "And these bits of paper are the prices, are they?"

"That's right," said Dilly, still smiling. "And you've got to give me some money." Dilly held his hand out.

Mother and Father laughed.

"That sounds fair enough," said Father. He looked at the things. "Umm . . . I'll have this book, and here's some pretend money for it."

Father smiled, and pretended to put some money into Dilly's hand.

Dilly stopped smiling.

"I don't want pretend money, Father," he said. "I want *real* money." Dilly snatched back the book that Father had picked up.

Father looked a little cross.

"Now, now, Dilly," said Father. "That isn't very nice. I've given you your pocket money, and you're not having any more today."

"But you said that you would give me money if I had a shop," he said. "This is my shop, and you've got to buy my things, and give me money."

Father looked even more cross.

"I'm afraid it doesn't quite work like that, Dilly," he said.

"Yes it does," said Dilly. He stamped his foot. "I want money!"

"Dilly," said Father, "I've told you once, and I've told you twice, you're not having any more money today!"

And then, of course, it happened. Dilly let loose with an ultra-special, 150-mile-per-hour super-scream, the sort that makes Father go white as a ghost, Mother feel ill, and me dive under the nearest piece of furniture.

Mother and Father told Dilly off, and then they explained that he wasn't old enough to have a proper shop and be given real money for his things. It was fine to play, they said, but that was all.

Later, when it was time for bed, Dilly started asking questions again.

"Father," he said, "about my shop."

"Yes, Dilly?" Father sighed.

"Well, if I have a real shop one day,

when I'm grown up . . ." he said.

"Yes, Dilly?"

"Well, if you come to buy something from my shop when I'm grown up . . ."

"Yes, Dilly?"

"Well, you will give me real money then, won't you . . . when I'm grown up?"

Father smiled.

"I should think so, Dilly," he said. "Now go to sleep."

And Dilly smiled too.

III.
DILLY AND THE DOCTORS GAME

Yesterday was a day I had really been looking forward to for ages. That's because my friend Deena was coming to play with me.

Deena goes to my school, and we always have lots of fun when we're together. In fact, Deena is my very best friend, and I really enjoy being with her.

I certainly enjoy Deena's company more than I do Dilly's when he's behaving badly. And that's exactly what he was doing yesterday, just before Deena arrived.

"Don't you dare touch that cupboard, Dilly," I heard Mother saying to him as I came down the stairs. I looked round the door and saw that Dilly was standing right next to the big cupboard where we keep a lot of toys.

"You got absolutely everything out of it this morning," Mother was saying, "and it took me ages to put it all back. I don't want you making any more mess this afternoon."

"But Mother," said Dilly, "I want to play with my favorite giant yellow eggshell."

"Well, I'm afraid you're just going to have to do without it for the rest of today, Dilly," said Mother. "I'll bet it's right at the bottom underneath everything else. Once you start pulling things out of that cupboard there's no stopping you."

"But Mother," said Dilly, "I *want* to play with my favorite giant yellow eggshell."

"Dilly," Mother said with a sigh, "I hope you're not going to be bad. I've told you over and over again that Dorla's friend Deena is coming to play, so you've got to be a well-behaved dinosaur this afternoon."

"That's not fair," said Dilly. "I want a friend to play with too!"

"Now, Dilly," said Mother, "it is fair, and you know it. Your friend Dixie came here to play just the other day. It's Dorla's turn today."

"But it isn't fair!" shouted Dilly, as he stamped his foot.

I knew this was going to happen.
Every time I have a friend round to
play, Dilly wants to play with us too.
But he always spoils our games, and I
tell him off, and then we argue and I
get told off and everything's ruined.

Just at that moment, the doorbell
rang, ding dong, ding dong. Deena
had arrived.

I took Deena straight up to my room
to play. Dilly was very cross for a

while, but then Mother said he could come and help her dig up the weeds in the garden. And Dilly just loves digging in the garden.

It was great playing with Deena. We played lots of different games, and then Deena had a very good idea.

"Hey, Dorla," she said. "Let's play doctors."

I love playing doctors. I've even got a little medical kit, with bandages, and a toy hammer for banging your knee, a thing to look in your ears and eyes and up your nose with, and a toy stethoscope.

We were having a marvelous time when all of a sudden we heard something, a noise that made the windows rattle, me wince and Deena dive under the bed.

"What was that?" she said when the

noise died down. She looked very pale.

Well, you and I know what it was, don't we? It was Dilly letting rip with an ultra-special, 150-mile-per-hour super-scream out in the garden. We heard the back door slam, and a stomp, stomp, stomp up the stairs, and Dilly's bedroom door slam so hard it sounded as if it were going to come through my wall.

Later, when Mother came up to give us a drink and a cookie, she said that Dilly had been very bad in the garden. He had pulled up the weeds she had shown him, but then he had also pulled up two of the new swamp-lilies that Father had just put in. Mother had told him off and said he had to go indoors. She had also said he wasn't to spoil our game, and that's when he had screamed.

Our doctors game was lots of fun,
but after a while we had a problem. I
had been the doctor first, and Deena
was the patient. Then I was the
patient, and Deena was the doctor.
But then we *both* wanted to be the
doctor. Who was going to be the
patient? We didn't know *what* to do.

Then we heard a stomp, stomp,
stomping noise along the landing
outside my bedroom door. The door
flew open and went BANG! against
the wall. And there was Dilly, looking
very mean.

"I want to play with you," he said. I could see he was all ready to make trouble if I said he couldn't play with us. But I didn't. I smiled at Deena, and Deena smiled at me.

"Okay, Dilly," we said together. "You can play with us."

Dilly looked surprised.

"You mean you're not going to send me out of your room?" he said.

"No," we said.

"And you're not going to tell Mother I'm spoiling your game?"

"No," we said.

"Oh," said Dilly, with a small smile. And then he shouted "Hurray!" as loud as he could, which is very, very loud.

Dilly was very good all through our game. He did everything that Deena and I asked him to, and he didn't do anything naughty, not even *once*.

Except for one thing, though . . . we pretended that we were putting him to bed, and we decided he needed a bedside cabinet to keep his medicine in. But we couldn't think of what to use.

"I know," said Dilly. "I know what we can use." He jumped up and ran out of my bedroom. We heard him go thud, thud, thud down the stairs. We heard a door open and go BANG! against the wall. Then it was quiet for a while.

And then there was the biggest noise we had heard all day.

CRASH!

It sounded as if everything had fallen out of a great big cupboard that was packed tight with things.

And that's exactly what had

happened. For when Dilly came thud, thud, thudding up the stairs again, can you guess what he was holding?

That's right, it was his favorite giant yellow eggshell!

"I thought we could use this," he said. "It will keep everything tidy."

"It's a shame you couldn't have thought about being tidy downstairs," said Mother, who was standing in the doorway behind Dilly. "I thought I told you not to pull all those toys out again! Who's going to tidy them up? That's what I want to know!"

I looked at Deena, and Deena looked at me.

"We'll help Dilly," we said. "He's been helping us with our game."

Mother smiled.

"Well, that's very nice of you, Dorla and Deena," she said. "Very nice indeed. And what about you, Dilly? Will you do some tidying up after you've finished the doctors game?"

Dilly thought for a while.

"All right, Mother," he said. "I'll

do some tidying up."

"Now there's a good dinosaur," said Mother, and went downstairs.

And do you know, when we came down to tidy up the toys, they were already in the cupboard. Mother told Dilly that the fairies had come and done it because he'd been so well-behaved.

But I don't know whether I believe her.

Do you?

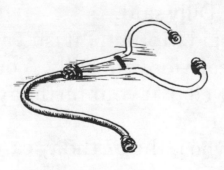

IV.   DILLY GOES TO THE DENTIST

One morning last week, the postman
put a letter through our door. Dilly got
to it before I did, and took it to
Mother.

"Is it a birthday card for me,
Mother?" Dilly said.

"No," said Mother, "it isn't a
birthday card for you, Dilly. You know
perfectly well that your birthday isn't
for ages yet."

"Well who is the birthday card for,

then?" said Dilly.

"It's not a birthday card at all,
Dilly," said Mother, a little crossly.
"And if you'd stop asking me
questions for a couple of seconds, I
could open it and find out what it is."

Mother opened the letter and read
it.

"Well?" said Dilly. "Is it for me?"

Mother sighed.

"No, Dilly," she said, "it isn't for
you. It's for Dorla. It's a letter from the
dentist saying that it's time she went
for a check-up again."

Dilly laughed and poked me in the
ribs.

"I bet the dentist will take all your
teeth out, Dorla," he said, "and you
won't be able to eat any of your food."

"No he will not," I said, and poked
Dilly back.

"All right, you two," said Mother and stepped between us. "That's enough of that. The dentist isn't going to take Dorla's teeth out, Dilly, because she's a good dinosaur and cleans her teeth twice a day, and she doesn't eat sugar cane all the time."

"So why does she have to go to the dentist?" said Dilly.

"To make sure that my teeth are okay, silly Dilly," I said.

"That's right, Dorla," said Mother. "and it's about time you went along for a check-up, too, Dilly. I'll make an appointment, and Father can take you with Dorla next week."

I looked at Dilly, and I could see that he didn't like what he had heard one bit.

"But I don't want to go to the dentist," he said, very quietly.

"Don't worry about it, Dilly," said Mother. "It will be all right. You're a good dinosaur who cleans his teeth twice a day, and you don't eat much sugar cane either. I'm sure there's nothing wrong with your teeth. But it's still a good idea to have a check-up."

But Dilly didn't really like the idea of going to a dentist at all. Every morning after that when he got up he said to Mother or Father: "It isn't today that I have to go to the dentist, is

it?'' And when they said it wasn't,
Dilly looked very relieved.

The day finally came.

"Come on, Dilly," said Father with
a big smile. "It's time to go to the
dentist."

Dilly didn't say anything. He just
looked at Father very stubbornly. In
fact he had his most stubborn face on,
the one that says: I'm-not-going-to-
do-whatever-it-is-you-want-me-to. I
could see we were going to have a few
problems.

"Come on, Dilly," said Father.
"I'm ready, Dorla's ready, and we're
both waiting for you."

Dilly didn't say anything.

"Now come on, Dilly," said Father.
"You're not being very sensible. Why
don't you put your coat on?" Father
held out Dilly's coat.

Dilly opened his mouth . . . and let go with an ultra-special, 150-mile-per-hour super-scream that was so loud it blew me into the kitchen and his coat, the one Father was holding, back on to the coat rack.

In the end, Father had to pick Dilly up and carry him out of the house under his arm. Even then Dilly held on to the rock by our front gate so hard

that Father nearly gave up and took him back indoors.

When we finally got to the dentist, Dilly looked very scared. The nice lady dinosaur behind the desk gave us both a coloring book and some crayons, but even that didn't make Dilly smile. He just sat there next to Father looking very green and frightened.

After a while it was our turn to go and see the dentist. I went in first, and Father came behind me, carrying Dilly under his arm.

"Hello, Dorla," said the dentist.

"I see you've brought your father and your little brother with you today." He smiled, "Who's first? You, or your brother, Dorla? Or perhaps it's your father!"

Father had put Dilly down. He was standing behind Father's legs, and

was peeping round at the dentist. As I
looked at him, he opened his mouth,
and I thought he was going to fire off
an ultra-special super-scream. He
thought he was too . . . but not a sound
came out. Dilly was so scared that
even his super-scream had gone into
hiding.

47

"Okay," said the dentist. "Why don't we show Dilly how easy it is, Dorla?"

I sat down in the big chair. I hadn't said anything, but I was a little nervous, too. Supposing I had to have something done? Supposing it hurt? The dentist was looking in my mouth . . . was everything all right?

It was.

"Your teeth are fine, Dorla, no problems at all," said the dentist. "Just keep brushing them, stay away from sweet things and you should be okay." He looked at Dilly, who was still standing behind Father and peeping round his legs.

"Now, Dilly," he said. "Are you ready for your turn?"

Dilly didn't say anything. He just looked more frightened than before.

"All right, then," said the dentist. "Perhaps you need to see someone else in the chair before you believe it won't hurt. How about Father?"

Father looked a little surprised.

"Come on, Mr Dinosaur," said the dentist. "When did you have your last check-up?"

"Er, I don't really remember," said Father. "Last year, I think . . ."

"Well it's about time for another one, then," said the dentist. Father sat down in the chair, and the dentist looked in his mouth.

"It's a good job you came today, Mr Dinosaur," said the dentist. "I think you've got a few problems in here . . ."

Anyway, it turned out that Father had a very bad tooth that needed filling. It took a long time, and although I couldn't be sure, I have a feeling that some of what the dentist did was painful for Father. But he wouldn't say so afterwards.

"Well, Dilly," the dentist said, "you see what can happen if you don't brush your teeth or if you eat too many sugar cane stalks! You end up having to have a filling like your father here."

Dilly, I noticed, didn't look frightened any more. In fact he looked very interested.

"Could I see what you've done in Father's mouth?" he said.

The dentist smiled.

"I'll tell you what, Dilly," he said. "I'll show you inside your father's mouth if you let me look in yours."

Dilly was quiet for a moment. Then he opened his mouth . . . and said:

"Okay."

So the dentist lifted Dilly up to look

50

inside Father's mouth, and then Dilly
sat in the chair while the dentist
looked in his.

"Well, Dilly," said the dentist after
a while, "your teeth are perfect. In fact
they're the nicest teeth I've seen for a
long time."

Dilly smiled.

"Better than Father's?" he said.

"Much better," said the dentist.

On the way home, Dilly couldn't stop smiling and laughing. He kept looking up at Father and bursting into giggles, and by the time we had got to our front door, Dilly and I could hardly keep from rolling on the floor, we were laughing so much.

Father didn't think it was very funny, although Mother did.

"You're a very naughty boy, Father," she said. "We'll have to make sure he doesn't eat too much sugar cane, won't we?"

Well, for the next few days Dilly kept telling everyone we met when we were out all about his trip to the dentist's. He made Mother wait at the Shopping Cavern checkout while he showed the lady his healthy teeth.

And he was so busy telling everybody about Father's bad teeth and giggling that he quite forgot to be badly-behaved for a couple of days.

But we all know that Dilly won't be a well-behaved dinosaur for long—don't we!